WALT DISNEY'S

LI'L WOLF and the
THREE LITTLE PIGS

GROLIER
BOOK CLUB EDITION

Early one day Li'l Wolf baked a cake.
The Big Bad Wolf came into the kitchen.
"Hi, Dad!" said Li'l Wolf.

"What's this?" asked the Big Bad Wolf.

"It is a cake for Practical Pig's
birthday party," said Li'l Wolf.

Now, the Big Bad Wolf was always trying
to catch Practical Pig and his brothers.

"I love parties!"
said the Big Bad Wolf.

"Sorry, Dad.
The three pigs
don't want you
at their party,"
said Li'l Wolf.
"So long, Dad!"

"I want to catch the three little pigs.
I must find a way to get into their house,"
the Big Bad Wolf said to himself.

"Aha!" he said.
"Li'l Wolf likes
cookies. I'll take
some to the party.
I'm sure the pigs
will let me in!"

The Big Bad Wolf
mixed flour, sugar,
and eggs in a bowl.

He stirred in
some milk and made
a pan of cookies.
"I hope this works,"
said the Big Bad Wolf.

The Big Bad Wolf put on his best coat.
He looked at himself in the mirror.
"How handsome I am!" he said.

Soon the cookies were baked.
They smelled delicious!
The Big Bad Wolf put them in a box.
Then he rode off on his bicycle
to the home of the three little pigs.

The three little pigs and Li'l Wolf
were busy eating the birthday cake.

"Look!" said one of the little pigs.
"Here comes Li'l Wolf's father, riding
down the street."

"I'm sure my father is up to no good,"
Li'l Wolf said. "We must be careful!"

The Big Bad Wolf knocked at the door.

Li'l Wolf came to the Dutch door.
"Look—cookies!" said the Big Bad Wolf.
"Thanks for the cookies, Dad. But
you can't come in. You will try to catch
the three little pigs," said Li'l Wolf.
Li'l Wolf closed and latched the door.

So the Big Bad Wolf went home.
He was not happy at all!
"I must think of another way
to catch those little piggies,"
said the Big Bad Wolf.

The Big Bad Wolf walked back and forth
in his house.

He tried to think of a new trick.

Soon he heard
a truck coming.
The Big Bad Wolf
got an idea.

"Package for you!" said the driver.

"May I borrow your hat, coat, and truck for a short time?" asked the Big Bad Wolf. "I want to have some fun with my friends."

"Sure," said the man. "I'll take a rest."

The Big Bad Wolf put on the man's hat
and coat.

He drove off in the delivery truck—
right to the house of the three pigs!

DAVE'S
DELIVERY
SERVICE

The Big Bad Wolf parked the truck
in front of the house.

He honked the horn loudly.

"Delivery for Practical Pig!"
called the Big Bad Wolf.

The three little pigs and Li'l Wolf
rushed to the window.

"Oh, look!" said one of the pigs.
"It must be a present for Practical Pig."

The four friends ran out of the house.
"Please help me with this big package,"
said the Big Bad Wolf.
He tried to sound like a delivery man.

But Practical Pig saw something strange.
"That's the Big Bad Wolf's tail! Quick,
back to the house!" said Practical Pig.

Li'l Wolf sighed.

"Dad, please don't try to catch my friends anymore. It's not nice," said Li'l Wolf.

"Hmmm…you are right, son," said the Big Bad Wolf.

The Big Bad Wolf crossed his fingers.
"I'll be good," he said to his son.
Li'l Wolf did not know his dad was lying!

"Thanks, Dad,"
said Li'l Wolf.
The Big Bad Wolf
drove away and
said to himself,
"I'm going to catch
those piggies!"

The Big Bad Wolf stood in his yard.
Soon Brer Bear came along.
He was pushing a hand cart.
"Hello there," said the Big Bad Wolf.
"How are you today?" asked Brer Bear.
Suddenly the Big Bad Wolf had a new idea.

"I need help," the Big Bad Wolf said.
"I have to get a big box to Practical Pig."

"I can wheel it over," said Brer Bear.

"Wonderful!" said the Big Bad Wolf.
"The package will be ready in an hour.
I'll leave it right here for you. Please
don't tell Practical Pig that I sent
the package. It's a surprise present
for his birthday."

Brer Bear left with his hand cart.
The Big Bad Wolf ran to the tool shed.
He found a huge box and some wood.
That was just what he needed!

The Big Bad
Wolf made a lid
from the wood.

He painted
pretty flowers
on the box.

Then he painted a sign
on one side of the box.
It read HAPPY BIRTHDAY.

HAPPY
BIRTHDAY

The Big Bad Wolf grabbed his fishing net.
He climbed into the box.
He pulled the lid down over himself.

But the Big Bad Wolf left a paw print
on the outside of the box!
Soon Brer Bear came back.

Brer Bear
lifted the box.
It was heavy.
He put it
on his cart.

Brer Bear pushed the cart
down the road to the house
of the three little pigs.

Li'l Wolf and his friends
were playing on the lawn.

"Look!" said Practical Pig.
"Brer Bear is coming this way
with a big box!"

Li'l Wolf and the three little pigs
gathered around the box.

"What's inside?" Li'l Wolf asked.

"This box is a present for you,
Practical Pig," said Brer Bear.

"Who sent it?" asked Practical Pig.
"I can't tell you," Brer Bear said.
"It's a surprise!"

Suddenly Practical Pig saw something
on the box—the Big Bad Wolf's paw print!
"Can you lift that heavy lid for me?"
Practical Pig asked Brer Bear.

"All right,"
said Brer Bear.
He wondered
what could be
in the box.

The Big Bad Wolf sat in the box.
He held on to his fishing net.
"I'll catch Practical Pig this time!"
the Big Bad Wolf said to himself.
Brer Bear lifted up the lid.

SWOOSH!
Down went the net—
on Brer Bear!
"Oh, my goodness!"
said the Big Bad Wolf.

HAPPY
BIRTHDAY

"Brer Bear looks very angry,"
said Practical Pig.

"He's ripped off the net,"
said the second pig.

"And he's picked up a branch,"
said the third pig.

Then Brer Bear chased the Big Bad Wolf down the road.

"That serves the Big Bad Wolf right!" said the three little pigs.

"I'm worried about my dad," Li'l Wolf said to the pigs. "I had better go home right away!"

Li'l Wolf went back to his house.

The Big Bad Wolf was sitting
in the kitchen.

He looked tired and unhappy.

"Dad, I brought you a piece of cake
from the party," said Li'l Wolf.